WOOF'S
SCARY
ADVENTURE

by Danae Dobson

Illustrated by Karen Loccisano

WORD PUBLISHING
Dallas · London · Sydney · Singapore

To my childhood friend, Holly Anne.
From tricycles and stuffed animals to boyfriends
and college life, you've always been special
to me. I'm thankful for the precious memories we've
shared through the years.

Woof's Scary Adventure
Copyright © 1991 by Danae Dobson for the text. Copyright © 1991 by Karen Loccisano for the illustrations.

Library of Congress Cataloging-in-Publication Data
Dobson, Danae.
    Woof's scary adventure / by Danae Dobson; illustrated by Karen
Loccisano.
       p.   cm. — (The Woof series ; 9)
    Summary: A tornado threatens Woof and his family, but another dog
in the neighborhood comes to Woof's rescue and God saves them all
from danger.
  ISBN 0-8499-0877-9
  [1. Tornadoes — Fiction. 2. Dogs — Fiction. 3. Christian life —
Fiction.] I. Loccisano, Karen, ill. II. Title. III. Series:
Dobson, Danae. The Woof series ; 9.
PZ7.D6614Ww 1991
[E] — dc20   90-27889
                                               CIP
                                               AC

Printed in the United States of America

1 2 3 4 5 6 9 AGH 9 8 7 6 5 4 3 2 1

A MESSAGE FROM
Dr. James Dobson

Before you read about this dog named Woof perhaps you would like to know how these books came to be written. When my children, Danae and Ryan, were young, I often told them stories at bedtime. Many of those tales were about pet animals who were loved by people like those in our own family. Later, I created more stories while driving the children to school in our car pool. The kids began to fall in love with these pets, even though they existed only in our minds. I found out just how much they loved these animals when I made the mistake of telling them a story in which one of their favorite pets died. There were so many tears I had to bring him back to life!

These tales made a special impression on Danae. At the age of twelve, she decided to write her own book about her favorite animal, Woof, and see if Word Publishers would like to print it. She did, and they did, and in the process she became the youngest author in Word's history. Now, thirteen years later, Danae has written eight more, totally new adventures with Woof and the Petersons. And she is still Word's youngest author!

Danae has discovered a talent God has given her, and it all started with our family spending time together, talking about a dog and the two children who loved him. We hope that not only will you enjoy Woof's adventures but that you and your family will enjoy the time spent reading them together. Perhaps you also will discover a talent God has given you.

The hands on the clock seemed to move extra slow. Mark Peterson yawned sleepily at his desk.

"School won't be out for another hour!" he thought.

He was trying to pay attention to Mrs. Thomas, but his mind kept wandering. He was thinking of cookies, baseball games, and his dog, Woof.

"Mark," Mrs. Thomas called out, "can you answer the question I asked?" Mark looked startled. He hadn't heard a word she said.

"I don't know," he replied. "I guess I wasn't listening very well."

Mrs. Thomas raised her eyebrows. "Pay closer attention, please."

"Yes, ma'am," Mark replied.

Just then, Mr. Hutchins, the school principal, came into the room. He whispered first to Mrs. Thomas, then turned and spoke to the class.

"Hello boys and girls," he said. "I have an important announcement. The weatherman says there is a chance we may have a tornado this afternoon. In case it does come, we must be prepared. I want everyone to quietly follow Mrs. Thomas. She will take you to the safest part of the building. Do exactly what she tells you to do."

Mark looked out the window. Sure enough, dark, threatening clouds were rolling across the sky.

Six-year-old Mark had never seen a tornado, but Grandma Peterson had told him about them. She said tornados are like big whirlwinds that move very fast. They often destroy trees and property. Sometimes even cars and houses get lifted off the ground! People have to go to cellars or basements for safety, because tornados are very dangerous.

Mrs. Thomas asked the class to listen carefully. Then she started calling names. "John, Julie, Mark . . . your mothers have come to take you home," she said. "Everyone else follow me."

Mark could see his mother standing in the hallway. He quickly gathered his things and went to meet her.

On their way down the hall, Mark's ten-year-old sister, Krissy, joined them. They hurried down the stairs and outside to the sidewalk.

Mrs. Peterson and the children began walking home. Clouds were boiling over their heads, and it was getting windy. Leaves and papers were tumbling down the street.

They finally arrived at their house. "We need to be careful in case a tornado does come," said Mother. "Let's go to the cellar for protection. Your father is on his way home from work. He'll be here shortly."

"We can't leave Woof outside!" said Mark. "I'll go get him." Quickly, Mark ran to the backyard to find his dog. There was no response. Mark then hurried inside the house.

"Woof!" he called, running from room to room. "Here boy!" but Woof did not come. Mark called his name again, but there was still no response.

"Where is Woof?" asked Krissy.

"I don't know, but he's not here!" exclaimed Mark. "Have you seen him, Mom?"

"No," Mrs. Peterson replied. "As a matter of fact, I haven't seen him all day. Go check the backyard one more time."

In a few minutes Mark returned, looking very un-happy. "Woof is gone!" he said sadly. "I've searched everywhere!"

"I'm sorry, Mark," said Mother. "But we really must go to the cellar. We'll wait there for your father."

It was almost an hour before Mr. Peterson got home.
By that time, the sky had become very dark. Lightning
flashed and thunder rolled through the clouds. Mark and
Krissy watched as Father struggled to get out of the car.
Even though he was tall and strong, he was barely able to
walk against the wind.

"Over here, Dad!" Mark called. "We're in the cellar!"

"Are you all right?" asked Krissy, holding the door open for him.

"I think so," said Mr. Peterson. "I sure am glad to be home. Traffic was horrible because of the storm. Is everything okay here?"

"Not really," answered Mark. "Woof is lost some-
where in the storm. I looked all around the house, but I
couldn't find him anywhere."

"Maybe he didn't hear us call his name," said Krissy.
"Can we go look for him again?"

"I'm sorry," replied Father. "It just isn't safe. We will
just have to be patient and wait here." Sadly, Mark and
Krissy obeyed their father and sat down.

They could hear tree limbs scraping against the house as
the wind howled outside.

"I'm so worried!" said Krissy. "I hope Woof is all right —
wherever he is!"

"God knows where Woof is right now," said Father. "More importantly, He has control over this storm, too. Remember the Bible story you learned in Sunday School? Jesus was in the boat with His disciples when a storm suddenly came. He just spoke the words, 'Peace be still,' and the wind and the waves obeyed Him. So you see, nothing is too difficult for God to handle."

"Let's pray for Woof," said Mother, "and about the storm." One by one, the Petersons asked God to take care of Woof. Then they prayed for their own safety.

Afterwards, everyone felt better, but they were still concerned. Mark and Krissy loved Woof very much. He was like a member of their family. They knew their special friend was out there lost, scared and alone.

And they were right!

On the corner of Maple Street a shaggy-haired dog was struggling against the wind. It was Woof! He had wandered several blocks from home and couldn't get back.

"Oh where are Mark and Krissy?" he thought. "How am I going to get home?" A huge tree fell beside him. He ran under the branches and huddled near the trunk. Woof didn't understand what was happening.

Back at the Petersons, Mark and Krissy were watching the storm. Father had opened the cellar door just enough to look out. Lightning flashed and thunder shook the ground. It began to pour down rain.

Suddenly, the wind grew stronger and the sky
became black. The Petersons could hear a loud roar, like
a freight train. Then they saw it!

"Look!" shouted Mark, "A tornado!" He pointed to a
funnel-shaped cloud in the distance.

"Yeah, and it's headed this way!" added Krissy.
Father quickly fastened the cellar door.

Woof peered out from under the branches of the tree. He could see the tornado, too. He didn't know what it was, but it frightened him. Where could he go? He knew he had to do something quick!

Just then, Woof heard a dog barking nearby. He noticed the sound was familiar. Anxiously, he strained to

see through the dust and trash in the air. Why, it was
Scruffy, his neighborhood friend. Scruffy was caught in
the storm, too, but he had found shelter under the porch
of an old house.

    Woof made his way to Scruffy's side. The two dogs
huddled close together and waited for the storm to pass.

Soon, the giant whirlwind began to move overhead. All kinds of things were flying through the air. Trash cans and even a bicycle were sucked up into the sky. Once, Woof felt like he was being pulled from under the porch! He was scared! He buried his head beneath his paws and closed his eyes. Was this ever going to end?

Just when he thought he couldn't take it anymore, the wind suddenly stopped. The tornado was gone! There was not a sound heard in the little city of Gladstone.

Woof and Scruffy cautiously left their hideaway and looked around. It was still raining but the clouds were lighter. Woof was so happy! He couldn't wait to go home to the Petersons and his nice, dry dog house.

But Woof had not forgotten what Scruffy had done for him. He nuzzled his little friend with his nose, then headed down the sidewalk. Scruffy looked happy, too, as he trotted off to his home on the next block.

All around the neighborhood, people were coming out of their cellars. And so did the Petersons. Mark and Krissy hardly noticed that their house had not blown away. They ran to the front yard, then to the back, looking for Woof.

"There he is!" shouted Mark. Woof was huddled on the back porch, wet and shivering. He was very happy to see the children. They ran and hugged him, rejoicing that he was home and safe. Mr. and Mrs. Peterson were also glad to see Woof. Mr. Peterson patted him on the head.

"We were worried about you, ol' boy!" he said kindly.

Mark and Krissy ran to get towels to dry Woof off. They fed him his dinner and mother laid a juicy steak bone in his bowl. But Woof didn't eat the special treat. "That's strange," said Krissy. "Woof has never turned down a steak bone before."

"He'll probably eat it later," said Father. "Let's go to bed now. It's been a long day."

Before Mark and Krissy went to sleep, they thanked
Jesus for protecting them from the storm. They also
thanked Him for taking care of Woof.

"It's nice to know God is in control," said Krissy.

"Yeah, even with something as big as a tornado,"
added Mark.

Much later, after everyone was asleep, Woof carried the bone to Scruffy's house. The little dog was asleep, so he quietly laid it in Scruffy's bowl. It was Woof's way of saying thanks for saving his life.

He looked for a moment at Scruffy, who was curled up in a little furry ball. Then he trotted home under the clear, starry sky.